The Chihuahua Chase

Also by A. E. Cannon

THE CHIHUAHUA CHASE

A. E. Cannon
Pictures by Julie Olson

Farrar Straus Giroux • New York

For Ruth,
with love
—A.E.C.

Text copyright © 2010 by A. E. Cannon
Pictures copyright © 2010 by Julie Olson
All rights reserved
Distributed in Canada by D&M Publishers, Inc.
Printed in October 2010 in the United States of America
by RR Donnelley & Sons Company, Harrisonburg, Virginia
First edition, 2010
3   5   7   9   10   8   6   4   2

www.fsgkidsbooks.com

Library of Congress Cataloging-in-Publication Data
Cannon, A. E. (Ann Edwards).
    The chihuahua chase / A.E. Cannon ; pictures by Julie Olson.— 1st ed.
        p.   cm.
    Summary: When Teddy's chihuahua Phantom goes missing, he and Addie May
join forces to try to figure out what happened to the dog.
    ISBN: 978-0-374-31259-6
    [1. Chihuahua (Dog breed)—Fiction.   2. Dogs—Fiction.   3. Lost and
found possessions—Fiction.   4. Interpersonal relations—Fiction.   5. Schools—
Fiction.   6. Mystery and detective stories.]   I. Olson, Julie, 1976– ill.   II. Title.

PZ7.C17135Cj 2010
[Fic]—dc22

                                                                    2008051441

The Chihuahua Chase

News line

Chihuahua Races to be held

SALT LAKE CITY—
The Rust Family Foundation has announced the first annual Chihuahua Race, to be held in Liberty Park this coming weekend. Proceeds will benefit several children's charities.

All local owners of Chihuahuas are invited to participate. Registration is limited to the first 150 dogs. Costumes are not required, although there will be a beauty pageant after the races.

Utah grou
win

St

By Ann

For the
PANGU
County
close to
Aug. 3
at the

T
th

1

Addie May Jones kicked a stone and sent it skittering down the sidewalk.

I wish that were Teddy's head, she thought.

Teddy Krebs was the meanest boy in the fourth grade. He was so mean that poison ivy plants would wilt if they saw him coming. If he got stuck in quicksand, the quicksand would spit him out. If hot lava were flowing toward him, the hot lava would stop dead at Teddy's feet. After that, the hot lava would turn around and flow back up the volcano.

Hot lava. Quicksand. Poison ivy. They were all afraid of Teddy Krebs.

Today at recess Teddy would NOT leave Addie May alone. He kept throwing the dodge ball at her. It was like he'd looked into a magic mirror before going to school and asked, "Mirror, mirror on the wall. Who should I smack with a rubber ball?"

The mirror had answered, "Addie May Jones." Obviously.

After chucking the dodge ball at her a billion times, Teddy stuck his freckled face in hers and said, "You're ugly."

"Ugly is as ugly does," said Addie May. Then she turned her back on Teddy and stalked away.

"Why don't you tell Mrs. Barnson?" Mimi, the Tattling Queen of the Fourth Grade, asked. Mrs. Barnson was their teacher and today's Recess Ranger.

Addie May shook her head. She could take care of herself! Besides, Addie May didn't like to tattle on other kids. Not even on people who deserved it. Such as Teddy, for example.

Mimi heaved a sigh of disgust. She trotted over to Mrs. Barnson, who busted Teddy on the spot.

Addie May could see the pleased look on Mimi's face as Teddy and Mrs. Barnson disappeared inside the school.

Later that day in the library, Teddy slipped Addie May a note that said *I'm sorry I hit you with a dodge ball. I wish I'd hit you with two dodge balls instead. Sincerely, Teddy Krebs.*

Addie May crumpled up the note and tossed it in the garbage can as Teddy watched, his arms folded across his chest and a sneer on his face. Yes! Perfect rim shot! Her big brother, Frank, would have been proud.

But now, as she was walking home from school, Addie May felt mad enough to spit. Not even the thought of the new Nancy Drew book (she loved Nancy Drew even more than she loved tropical-fruit-flavored Skittles) in her backpack made her feel better.

WHAT WAS WRONG WITH TEDDY?

Why couldn't he find another girl to torture? Mimi, for example. No one—probably not even Mrs. Barnson or the principal—would mind if Teddy started torturing Mimi.

Addie May turned the corner and headed up First Avenue. Birds sang happy songs in the branches overhead.

Duh! Of course they sang happy songs! They were birds and that's what birds do! Also, they didn't have Teddy Krebs throwing dodge balls at their heads during recess! Addie May kicked another stone.

"Oh!"

Addie May jerked her head up to see who had spoken.

It was the Ghost Lady!

At least that's what Frank called her, because the Ghost Lady looked like a drawing done with a gray crayon. Her hair was gray and her clothes were gray, and she was so wispy that if the wind blew, you were afraid she would flutter away and get stuck in some treetops. The gray lady lived by herself in an apartment building on First Avenue. Addie May used to help Frank deliver newspapers there. The Ghost Lady never spoke to them, but she always left Frank generous tips.

"I'm so sorry," said Addie May. "Did my rock hit you?"

"Don't worry. I'm fine," the Ghost Lady answered in a gray, whispery voice. Then she hurried off.

"Sorry," Addie May called after her again.

The Ghost Lady didn't look back. If anything, she moved away faster.

She's probably afraid I'll kick another rock at her, Addie May thought with a sigh.

Stupid awful Teddy Krebs. *Everything* was his fault!

"Chihuahua races?" Dad said as he set the dinner table. "What will they think of next?"

Mom opened the oven door to check on the roasting chicken. "We had a good laugh about it down at the paper today."

Mom worked as a crime reporter at the *Deseret News*. Dad taught P.E. and coached football at West High School.

Addie May perked up at the mention of Chihuahuas as she plunked ice cubes into the water pitcher.

Her aunt Gabby, who lived in Los Angeles, had a Chihuahua named Vince. Vince wore a purple collar and did tricks such as walking on his front legs with his back legs sticking up in the air. Aunt Gabby loved Vince so much she had his name tattooed on her ankle.

Addie May loved Vince, too, which is why she asked for a Chihuahua every Christmas. She never got one—just notes from her parents (ho ho ho!) pretending to be Santa Claus.

Dear Addie May, the notes always read, *I'd love to bring you your own Chihuahua this year but (sadly) Chihuahuas make your father sneeze . . .*

It was true. Any time Dad got around Vince—

or any dog except for poodles—he started wheezing and his eyes got as puffy as marshmallows.

"I can't believe you want a Chihuahua, Addie May," said Frank. Frank was supposed to be tearing up lettuce for a salad. Instead he sat at the snack bar, sipping a Coke. "They look like rats with bat ears."

"They do not look like rats," said Addie May. "Or bats."

"Yeah, you're right," said Frank. "Rats and bats are MUCH better-looking."

Frank fake-laughed at his own stupid joke.

"Leave your sister alone," Mom said to Frank. She turned to Addie and Dad. "One of the local TV stations is doing a promotion for the races at Liberty Park tonight. Interested owners and their Chihuahuas are invited to show up for a free trial run."

"Can I go?" Addie May asked.

Frank jumped off the snack bar and draped a big arm around Addie May. He gave her a friendly noogie. "Josh and I are playing tennis at the park tonight. You can catch a ride with us."

Addie May smiled to herself. Maybe this day would turn out to be okay after all—in spite of Teddy Krebs!

2

Addie May could not believe it.

Everywhere she looked there were Chihuahuas. Black ones. Tan ones. White ones. It was as though someone had opened up a big bag of Chihuahua M&M's and sprinkled a heap of them in this corner of the park.

Most of the dogs were held by their owners, who stood around a small track divided by ropes into five straight lanes. A TV reporter asked them questions while a cameraman filmed their answers. When it was their turn, people stepped up to the starting chutes and waited for the signal. Then they let go of their little dogs, who streaked down the track for the finish line.

Or not.

Some of the dogs just stood at the starting line and shivered. Some of the dogs charged halfway down the lane, then changed their minds. They turned around, raced back, and jumped straight into their owners' laps.

But some of the dogs ran like tiny racehorses.

Especially a dog named Tex.

People were talking about Tex as Addie May weaved her way through the crowd.

"Did you see him move?"

"That little dog hasn't lost a race tonight!"

"Who is this Tex dog anyway?"

"Is it true that Bobby 'the Car Guy' Rust owns him? If I remember right, the Rust family is sponsoring the races."

Addie May stopped dead in her tracks when she heard the name *Bobby Rust*. Bobby Rust owned about a million car dealerships in the city. He starred in his own car commercials and his picture was on bus posters that said NEED A CAR? THEN TRUST RUST!

He also owned apartment buildings all over Salt Lake City, including the building where Frank used to deliver newspapers.

Bobby Rust was as rich as the Queen of England, only better-looking. His wife and kids were better-looking, too.

Even though he was rich, Bobby Rust's kids

went to public school just like normal kids. People always said how amazing it was that the Rusts weren't snobs. In fact, Bobby Rust's son, Zack, was a sixth grader at Wasatch Elementary, where Addie May went.

Zack Rust.

Just thinking about him made Addie May feel all fluttery inside. Zack had smiled at her in the cafeteria right before Christmas, even though he was in the sixth grade and she was in the fourth.

Addie May had been drawing little hearts in her notebook that said *ZR + AMJ* ever since.

"Who's ZR?" Frank asked one night as he peeked over Addie May's shoulder. Addie May clobbered him hard with her notebook.

This was the first time she'd ever really liked a boy, and for sure she didn't need a big brother to bug her about it!

Addie May craned her neck, searching through the throng of Chihuahua owners. Was Zack here tonight?

"Next up!" the man in charge boomed.

Addie May's heart thumped as Zack stepped out of the crowd, holding a sleek black-and-tan Chihuahua. It was, in fact, the best-looking dog Addie May had ever seen. Same with Zack. He

was the best-looking boy Addie May had ever seen.

What should she do? Wave at him? Or duck behind the large man standing next to her?

She stood frozen.

"Who'd like to take on this evening's reigning champion?" the man in charge announced.

Zack searched the crowd, looking for a challenger. His eyes passed right over Addie May. He didn't even see her!

"Wait up!" came a voice. "What's going on here?"

There was jostling as the crowd parted and a boy appeared.

Addie May gasped. Her stomach plunged to her knees—sort of like the *Titanic* plunging to the bottom of the ocean.

No! It wasn't possible!

Walking toward Zack was Teddy Krebs, holding the world's homeliest Chihuahua.

"Hey, everybody," said Teddy. "Meet Phantom."

3

How homely was Phantom?

If there was a Chihuahua beauty pageant, Phantom wouldn't be allowed to enter. If a bunch of girl Chihuahuas decided to rate a bunch of boy Chihuahuas for fun, they wouldn't even bother with Phantom. If Phantom wanted a makeover, the makeover lady would say, "Sorry, Charlie! No can do!"

Phantom was neither tan nor black—just some homely color in between. His snout was flatter than it should have been, as though he'd run into a wall and forgotten to straighten his nose out afterwards. One of his ears (which were both too big) flopped over, and there were scars that looked like tattoos on Phantom's skull and chest.

"We were out for a walk and wanted to see what all the fuss was about," Teddy said.

The man in charge gave Phantom a doubt-ful look. But Zack smiled (like a movie star!) and explained all about the races.

"We're in," said Teddy.

Phantom gave a happy yelp.

Zack and Teddy and their dogs took their places at the starting chutes. Addie May felt a lit-tle light-headed as she noticed how the late after-noon sun shone on Zack's golden hair.

"On your mark . . ."

Teddy whispered something in Phantom's ear.

"Get set . . ."

Zack whispered something in Tex's ear.

"STOP!"

Stop? Zack and Teddy looked up at the man in charge, who was as surprised as they were by the interruption. Who had yelled "Stop"?

A woman with tight curly hair shoved and pushed her way to the starting line. She was carrying a huge sign that said STOP THE MADNESS!

Addie May saw the TV reporter say something to his cameraman.

"Excuse me," said the man in charge coldly. "What do you think you're doing?"

The woman answered with an unfriendly smile. "You'll find out soon enough."

She waved at the TV reporter, motioning him to join her. Then she made an announcement.

"My name is Sondra Hopkins, and I am president of Save the Chihuahuas." She waved her sign. "I'm here to protest cruelty to animals in general and to Chihuahuas in particular."

No one moved. No one said anything, except for Tex, who whimpered again.

"See what I mean?" Sondra Hopkins boomed, and she pointed at Tex, who leaped into Zack's arms and shivered. "This poor little darling here is scared to death!"

"Duh," Teddy said. "He's scared of you."

Everyone laughed. Even the TV reporter and his cameraman. Sondra Hopkins, president of Save the Chihuahuas, turned red as rubies. She narrowed her eyes into slits like a snake. They glittered at Teddy.

"You'll be sorry for this," she said.

She looked at the camera again. "Turn that stupid thing off!"

Sondra Hopkins glared at Teddy one last time before stomping off.

"As I was saying before we were so rudely

interrupted," said the man in charge, "on your mark . . ."

Zack and Teddy lined up their dogs.

"Get set . . ."

The camera crew turned on their lights and started recording.

"GO!"

Tex and Phantom were off!

Tex took an early lead. No surprise there. But within seconds, Phantom had gained on Tex, and the two little dogs raced neck and neck like Beauty and the Beast.

"Wow!"

"Look at 'em go!"

"I never knew small dogs could move so fast!"

Addie May listened to the comments around her as she watched Tex and Phantom streak for the finish line.

"Go, Tex!"

"Go, Phantom!"

"Win one for the Gipper!"

"Who's the Gipper?"

Addie May's heart was pounding. Which dog would win?

Faster and faster. Neck and neck. It was a race to the finish.

"AND THE WINNER IS . . . PHANTOM!" announced the man in charge.

The crowd burst into noisy cheers.

"Yay for Phantom!"

"Phantom rocks!"

"Phantom is the Man!"

"No way! Phantom is the Dog!"

Addie May watched Teddy scoop up Phantom in his arms and hold him high in the air like a dog trophy. If Madame President of Save the Chihuahuas Sondra Hopkins were around, she'd probably complain that Teddy was giving Phantom a fear of heights.

Zack, looking stunned by his loss, tucked Tex into his arms. He walked over and shook Teddy's hand.

That Zack, thought Addie May, *has real class. Not like Teddy.*

"Good trial run, boys," said the man in charge. "We expect both of you to be here for the real race this weekend! Zack's dad will be our master of ceremonies."

Zack and Teddy nodded hard. Then Teddy held Phantom in the air again while people clapped.

Addie May turned to go. She didn't want to

run into either Zack or Teddy. She turned to get one last look at Zack. But instead she saw Teddy.

When he thought no one was watching, he dropped a quick kiss on Phantom's head.

4

Addie May found herself thinking about Zack and Teddy the next morning as she ate her oatmeal. She thought about them during school when she was supposed to be paying attention to Mimi's oral report on Sedimentary Rocks and Why We Need Them. She thought about them as she walked home from school, kicking rocks.

She always started out thinking about Zack. But somehow she always ended up thinking about Teddy.

Addie May was confused. What kind of boy went around kissing dogs? Could it be that Teddy wasn't so mean after all?

Addie May was still thinking about Teddy and Phantom as she rode her bike to the playground, where she was meeting friends to play soccer. Tulips as pink as lipstick were blooming everywhere. Spring had come to Salt Lake City! The warm breeze tickled her face and ruffled her hair. Addie May loved how free riding her bike always made her feel . . .

"SCRAM!"

An angry voice startled Addie May. Her bike wobbled, and she nearly toppled over. Addie May stopped and saw a bald man with arms as thick as hams watering his front yard. He wore a T-shirt that said SOMETIMES I WAKE UP GRUMPY. OTHER TIMES I LET HIM SLEEP.

"I SAID BEAT IT!"

The man scowled in her direction. Was he scowling at her?

No. He was scowling at the lilac bushes lining his driveway. He pointed the garden hose at them and sprayed.

Addie May heard a yelp. A little dog with one floppy ear shot out from beneath the lilacs like a Fourth of July bottle rocket.

Addie May gasped. Could it be? The little dog looked just like . . .

"Phantom! Come here, boy!"

Teddy Krebs rounded the corner and ran toward Phantom, whistling. Phantom shook the water off his back and ran toward Teddy. Then

he leaped straight into Teddy's outstretched arms.

What were Teddy and Phantom doing in Addie May's neighborhood?

"THIS IS YOUR LAST WARNING!" the man shouted at Teddy. "KEEP YOUR MUTT OFF MY PROPERTY OR YOU'LL BOTH BE SORRY!"

Teddy was shaking. His face looked like a red balloon ready to pop.

The man sprayed an arc of water in Teddy's direction and scowled again. Then he threw down the hose, turned off the faucet, and stomped inside his house.

"You leave us alone!" Teddy shouted. But it was too late. The front door was already shut.

"Wow," Addie May said.

Teddy turned and saw Addie May for the first time.

"How long have you been there?" Teddy snarled at her.

Addie May bristled.

"None of your beeswax," she shot back.

Teddy opened his mouth—no doubt to say something rude. But Phantom squirmed up his chest and licked Teddy on his chin. Teddy smiled.

In spite of herself, Addie May smiled, too.

"Who was *that*?" Addie May nodded at the man's house.

"Our new neighbor," Teddy answered. "He hates dogs."

Addie May blinked. "You live around here?"

It was true that Teddy was in her class at school. But she had no idea he lived so close to her.

"We do now." Teddy shrugged, then pointed. "Me and my dad and Phantom—we moved into that apartment building this week."

It was the same apartment building where Addie May used to help Frank deliver newspapers—the same apartment building where the Ghost Lady lived.

Addie May looked up and saw a curtain in a third-story window move.

Was someone in the apartment building spying on her and Teddy and Phantom? Just as suddenly, the curtain dropped. Addie May frowned a little to herself.

"Is that your bike?" Teddy asked her.

Addie May nodded.

"Yeah?" Teddy snorted. "Well, it's just the kind of bike a nerd like you would like."

Addie May glared at Teddy as she crawled back on her bike.

"Loser," she said.

Teddy let out an unfriendly laugh as Addie May pushed off and pedaled for the school yard.

And to think for a minute there she'd begun to believe Teddy Krebs could actually be nice!

Just goes to show, thought Addie May, *how wrong, wrong, wrong you can be about a person sometimes.*

5

The next day, Addie May ignored Teddy at early recess when he told her she had fleas.

She ignored him at lunch when he asked if she wanted some "seafood," then showed her the mashed potatoes in his mouth and shouted, "SEE FOOD! Get it?"

She ignored him during math when he said she was as smelly as wet socks on a warm day.

Shortly after the "smelly socks" remark, the school secretary, Mrs. Thompson, walked into the classroom and handed Mrs. Barnson a slip of paper.

"Teddy, will you please go with Mrs. Thompson?"

"I hope you get in big fat serious trouble," Addie May whispered as he brushed past her.

Teddy was gone for fifteen minutes. When he returned, his face was so white even his freckles had disappeared. What was going on?

He dropped a note on Addie May's desk as he walked back to his seat. Addie May stuffed it in her Nancy Drew paperback before Mrs. Barnson or anyone else had a chance to see it.

Addie May thought about ignoring the note just like she'd been ignoring everything else about Teddy that day. But she couldn't.

Addie May was a sucker for notes.

She loved writing them. (She had lots of colored gel pens for writing and decorating purposes.) She also loved reading notes. She especially liked reading notes written to other people besides herself.

She always read the notes girls sent Frank because Frank just left them lying around the house like they were his shoes and socks. Big brothers could be so messy sometimes!

Mom had caught her reading some of Frank's notes once.

"Addie May," she said sternly. "Stop being so snoopy!"

Ashamed, Addie May crumpled up the notes and dropped them in the nearby wastebasket. As she left the room, she saw Mom reach for the garbage can herself.

Addie May smiled. She came by her talent for snooping naturally. Obviously.

Snooping was a good talent for a crime reporter to have. It was also a good talent for a detective, which is what Addie May wanted to be.

When no one was looking, Addie May took Teddy's note from the back of her book. Then she opened it. Carefully. Who knew? Maybe there was a black widow spider tucked inside.

But no. There was only Teddy's rough handwriting.

I need help, the note read. *Meet me on the playground at 5:30 this afternoon. Please.*

Teddy needed help? From her? Why? What was going on?

Addie May put down the note and scrunched up her face. Of course it was a trick. Addie May would show up and Teddy wouldn't be there. Or if he was, he'd be hiding with a pile of rotting chestnuts, ready to chuck them at her.

Still. He'd said please.

She sighed and crammed the note in her back pocket. She knew where she would be this afternoon at five-thirty.

Addie May checked her watch again.

Five-fifty p.m.

She knew it! Teddy wasn't coming! It had been a trick all along! A mean, stupid, no-good, lousy, Teddy Krebs kind of trick.

I can't believe I fell for it!

Disgusted, Addie May picked up a loose clump of grass and threw it. She got up from the school soccer field where she'd been waiting and stomped toward her bike.

"Hey! Hold on! Don't leave yet!"

Addie May turned to see Teddy huffing and puffing across the playground, clutching a stack of papers in his hand.

Addie May folded her arms across her chest and scowled.

"You're late," she said when Teddy joined her.

Instead of apologizing, Teddy thrust a pile of papers under Addie May's nose.

"It took me longer than I thought it would to run these off."

Still scowling, Addie May took one.

There was a large picture of Phantom staring straight into the camera with red laser-beam eyes

31

caused by the flash. Underneath the picture was the word REWARD!

Reward? Addie May gasped and looked up at Teddy, who nodded grimly.

"Phantom's gone," he said. "Dad called me at school when he came home for lunch."

"Oh," cried Addie May, "this is horrible!"
She read on.

MISSING: One Chihuahua
NAME: Phantom
DESCRIPTION: Good-looking with one floppy ear

IF YOU HAVE ANY INFORMATION, PLEASE CONTACT LYLE OR TEDDY KREBS

At the bottom, the flyer listed Teddy's phone number.

"What happened?" Addie May asked.

"Dad thinks maybe Phantom got out when the superintendent showed up to fix our disposal."

"Have you talked to the superintendent yet?"

Teddy shot Addie May a withering look. "Duh. How stupid do you think I am?"

"I don't think you're stupid," Addie May snapped. "Just rude."

Teddy shrugged his shoulders. "Whatever."

A moment of silence passed between them. Addie May thought about getting on her bike and leaving. But whenever she looked at Phantom's picture, the dog's laser-beam eyes pleaded, "Help me! Help me!"

Addie May sighed. "What did the superintendent say?"

"He said he didn't think that Phantom got out of the apartment . . ."

Teddy looked just like Addie May's mother looked whenever Frank said he didn't have any homework.

"But you don't believe him?"

"Mr. Covey is a really nice old man," Teddy said. "Dad and I like him a lot. But I think he knows something he's not telling us."

For the first time, Teddy looked like any other kid who's just lost a dog—sad and even a little scared. It was as though a mask had fallen from his face.

"I'm going to put these flyers up around the neighborhood," Teddy said.

"Well," said Addie May slowly, "before you do that, I think the two of us ought to pay a visit to the superintendent."

6

With his snowy beard and mustache, his rosy cheeks and twinkling blue eyes, Mr. Covey, the superintendent, looked like Santa Claus. He wore a red work shirt and overalls covered in sawdust.

"Come in, come in," Mr. Covey said with a warm smile when Addie May and Teddy knocked on his door.

The inside of Mr. Covey's apartment was cramped but tidy. A large tool chest stood in the corner. Overstuffed chairs, covered with knit afghans, surrounded a small TV. The coffee table held photo albums and crossword puzzle magazines.

"Sit down. Please make yourselves comfortable," said Mr. Covey. "Can I get you something to drink? Ice water? Orange juice? Root beer?"

"Root beer for me, please," said Addie May.

"Me, too," said Teddy.

"Good call," said Mr. Covey. "I always say life goes down easier with a cold mug of root beer."

Addie May watched the old man shuffle off to the kitchen. Teddy was right. Mr. Covey was very nice. Then why didn't Teddy believe him about Phantom?

A few minutes later, Mr. Covey returned with drinks and a small plate of Oreo cookies on a tray. He set them down on the coffee table.

"Help yourselves, kids."

Teddy reached for an Oreo and unscrewed it—just the way Addie May always did. He licked the creamy center before popping a cookie half in his mouth—just the way Addie May did, too.

"Now," Mr. Covey said, taking a seat, "what can I do for you two?"

"It's about Phantom," Teddy said, dusting cookie crumbs off his face.

"Your little dog?" Mr. Covey looked very concerned.

Teddy nodded, and Mr. Covey shifted in his seat as though it were hot. Could it be that Mr. Covey was nervous?

"We want to ask you a few questions," Addie May said, watching Mr. Covey closely.

"That would be fine." Mr. Covey gave her a smile. A *weak* smile, Addie May noted.

"You visited the Krebses' apartment this morning, right?" she asked.

Mr. Covey nodded. "Mr. Krebs asked me to take a look at the kitchen sink while he was at work." He turned to Teddy. "By the way, how is your disposal working?"

Teddy nodded. "It works great."

Mr. Covey looked pleased. "People always say I have a way with disposals."

Disposals? Addie May wanted to scream. Instead, she politely but firmly asked her next question.

"Did you see Phantom when you went into the Krebses' apartment?"

"Yes," Mr. Covey said. "He was asleep on the couch when I let myself in."

"Was he still there when you left?"

Mr. Covey paused. "Yes. I'm sure he was."

Why had Mr. Covey hesitated?

"Are you positive?" Addie May pressed.

Mr. Covey nodded.

"Is it possible you left the door open when you left?"

"I always lock up when I leave." Mr. Covey looked at Teddy. "I feel real bad about Phantom. I had a Chihuahua once named Moki. He used to wake me up at six a.m. every morning. Best darn dog I ever had. Best darn alarm clock I ever had, too."

Mr. Covey sounded sincere. No doubt about it. What was going on here?

Mr. Covey glanced at the stack of fliers in Teddy's hand. "Can I help you with those?"

"Yeah, thanks." Teddy peeled some papers off the pile and passed them along to Mr. Covey.

"Nice picture," Mr. Covey said after whistling in admiration. "He looks mighty handsome."

"Dad and I found him at the pound," said Teddy. "I got him for Christmas."

"Lucky for Phantom," said Mr. Covey. "Lucky for you."

Teddy nodded.

"This is hard, isn't it, son?" said Mr. Covey.

Teddy swallowed and blinked.

"Have faith," said the old man. "I'm guessing you'll find him."

7

So what do you think about Mr. Covey?" Teddy asked Addie May as they walked out of the apartment building.

"I think he looks like Santa Claus," said Addie May.

Teddy laughed as the two of them walked back to the school. It was the first time Addie May remembered him laughing *with* her—not *at* her.

"I also agree with you," Addie May said. "He isn't telling us everything."

Teddy heaved a sigh. "I like Mr. Covey. He's real good to all the people in the building. I don't want him to be the bad guy."

Addie May reached down, plucked a blade of grass, and chewed on the end of it thoughtfully.

"Teddy, you said your dad found Phantom at the pound. Did you call the pound to see if he'd been picked up?"

"Duh," he said. "Right after I called Mr. Covey."

"So what did they say?"

"That they didn't have any Chihuahuas with floppy ears." Teddy kicked an empty soda can hard and watched it bounce down the sidewalk.

"Has Phantom ever run off before?"

"Phantom does love to run." Teddy cocked his head in thought. "Sometimes he'll sneak out the door and race up and down the hallway. And when we go for walks outside, I take off the leash so he can run ahead. But he always comes straight back when I call. He's as smart as he is fast."

Addie May thought if there was a bumper sticker about a person's Chihuahua being smarter than another person's honor roll student, Teddy would slap that one on the family car.

Addie May and Teddy spent the next hour trudging through the neighborhood, tacking up posters on telephone poles. They even left one at the Sweet Branch Library and Eighth Avenue Market.

When they were done, they bought themselves treats at the neighborhood 7-Eleven and sat on the grass out front.

"All these posters have got to help," Addie May said after taking a sip of her wild cherry Slurpee.

"I hope so." Teddy didn't sound convinced.

"What do you think has happened to Phantom, Teddy?"

Teddy's face grew very serious. "The truth?"

Addie May nodded.

"I think that Phantom's been dognapped."

Chills chased each other down Addie May's arms. She couldn't say why, exactly. But she was afraid that Teddy was right.

"Okay, so this is what we do next," Addie May said briskly. Coming up with plans always made Addie May feel better. "We'll both go home and draw up a list of suspects. Then we'll put our lists together tomorrow." She paused. "After school."

Addie May added the "after school" part so no one would get the wrong idea about her and Teddy Krebs.

Especially Zack Rust. No point in giving Zack Rust the wrong idea about anything.

Teddy was looking at her like he could read her mind, and Addie May squirmed.

"Whatever," he sneered.

Addie May blushed. She would dearly love to slap that sneer clean off Teddy's freckled face.

"Why did you ask me to help you anyway?" she said coldly.

"Because you're always checking out mysteries when our class goes to the library," Teddy answered. "And this a mystery."

Addie May was surprised. Who'd think Teddy Krebs would notice what kind of books she liked?

"Well," she said, "I do love mysteries."

"That's because you're a nerd," Teddy said.

"That's it!" said Addie May. "I've had it with you!"

She dumped the rest of her Slurpee on the grass, threw away the cup, and marched to her bike. She got on and rode away without looking back.

"NERD!" Teddy's voice came whistling on the wind after her.

8

W hy the sour face tonight?" Dad asked Addie May as the family sat around the dinner table.

Addie May stabbed her grilled chicken breast with a fork. "I'm thinking about Teddy Stupid Krebs!"

"Addie . . ." Mom scolded gently.

"It's true, Mom! He's totally stupid! After everything I did to help him this afternoon, he called me a nerd."

Mom looked interested as she helped herself to the salad. "Help him? Why? What's going on?"

Addie May told everyone about Phantom and the reward posters and old Mr. Covey. Mom frowned a little.

"This is so strange," she said. "There's been a

rash of Chihuahua disappearances in the Salt Lake Valley this past month. Officer Williams was telling us about it just this afternoon."

Officer Williams was a friend of Mom's. He kept her and the other crime reporters at the paper updated on breaking news stories.

"How many Chihuahuas are we talking about here?" Dad was curious.

"Six or seven. Something like that," Mom answered.

"It's probably the city rat catcher," said Frank. "He got mixed up and thought the dogs were rats." Frank did an imitation of a city rat catcher. "Lookee here! I got me a truckload of yapping rats!" Frank barked.

Mom and Dad laughed, but Addie May shot Frank an evil look.

"Excuse me. Am I the only one who finds it strange that our city's Chihuahua population is disappearing from right under our very noses?" Addie May asked.

Dad buttered a roll. "Hold up, Addie May. I'm sure there are still plenty of Chihuahuas in Salt Lake City to go around. More than enough, in fact. My guess is that they'll all come home, wagging their tails behind them."

Dad sneezed, just thinking about all those Chihuahuas.

"Dad's right," said Mom. "It's probably just a coincidence. Still. It is an odd one . . ."

• • •

Odd? Addie May thought to herself as she opened her math book and started her homework later that night. So many disappearing Chihuahuas was downright bizarre!

Addie May read the instructions on the top of page 149. *Put the decimal in the proper place . . .*

Decimals? Who cared about stupid decimals when there were Chihuahuas disappearing?!

Instead of copying down the problem, Addie May began doodling on her math paper. She wrote out the following questions.

WHAT'S HAPPENING?
WHO'S RESPONSIBLE?
WHY ARE THEY DOING IT?
HOW ARE THEY DOING IT?

Those were the questions Addie May's mother always asked whenever she wrote a story for the newspaper. It was a crime reporter's job to ask questions and dig up the answers. Maybe if Addie May thought like a crime reporter, she'd discover what had happened to Phantom.

She looked over the questions again, then began jotting notes.

WHAT'S HAPPENING? In the past month, a number of Chihuahuas have mysteriously disappeared, including Phantom (owned by Teddy Krebs).

Addie May put down her pencil and remembered the way Teddy had called her a nerd that afternoon. She was pretty sure Zack would never have treated her that way. Zack would have thanked her. Maybe even expressed his gratitude by buying her a new pen from the pen dispenser in the main office. She'd let him buy her the purple pen with sparkles.

Did Addie May really want to help Teddy?

The answer was no.

Did she want to help Phantom?

Sighing, Addie May picked up her pencil and wrote the next question.

WHO'S RESPONSIBLE? Someone who wants to rid the world of Chihuahuas?

Addie May put down her pencil again and remembered all those Chihuahuas at the time trials at Liberty Park. She smiled to herself. Seriously, who could hate a Chihuahua? They were so cute, with their tiny paws and big eyes and

their long tails that curled up at the end. What was not to like?

No doubt about it, Chihuahuas were way lovable, which is why people went nuts over them. Like Aunt Gabby in Los Angeles, for example. Aunt Gabby loved Vince more than some people love their own kids.

And what about that lady in Liberty Park the night of the time trials? The one who showed up with signs that said SAVE THE CHIHUAHUAS? Now there was someone who really, really, REALLY loved Chihuahuas.

Suddenly, Addie May's scalp tingled, the way it always did when an idea struck her.

"Oh my gosh," Addie May said out loud. "OH MY GOSH!"

What if the person responsible for the dognappings (and this was a case of dognapping, Addie May felt sure) wasn't a Chihuahua hater after all? What if she was a Chihuahua lover? And what if that person thought she was taking those dogs to a better home? Her home, for example?

Addie May tingled all over now as she remembered what the woman had said to Teddy Krebs.

You'll be sorry for this.

Could it be she was trying to get even with Teddy by rescuing Phantom?

Addie May shot out of her chair and began pacing as she searched her brain. *What was the woman's name? It started with an "H," didn't it? Hopper? Hop-a-Long? Hop-a-Lot? Hop-Until-You-Drop? Something like that? Oh, WHAT was that lady's name?*

Maybe she could find a Web site for Save the Chihuahuas. Surely the name would be there.

Addie May bolted out of her room and into the family room, where Frank was already on the computer.

"I need the computer," Addie May said. "This is very, very important, FYI."

"You can have it after I'm done," Frank said. "I'm doing homework, FYI. Which is also very, very important."

The computer gave a friendly chime.

"YOU ARE NOT DOING HOME-WORK!" Addie May shouted. "YOU ARE INSTANT-MESSAGING SOMEONE!"

"Yes. I'm a freaking genius. I'm instant-messaging WHILE I'm doing my homework," said Frank. "I'll be off in an hour."

"MOM!" Addie May called.

"Too bad, so sad," said Frank. "She's gone. Dad, too."

Addie May felt like her hair was on fire, she was so mad. If she were Frank's size, she'd toss him to the ground. She'd pinch his arm and pummel him on the chest. Then she'd get on the computer and send her own instant message to Frank's friend. *Can't talk. Have to go watch* Sesame Street *now! Sincerely, Frank "the Cookie Monster" Jones.*

She stormed out of the room and into the kitchen.

What should she do next?

The telephone rang and Addie May snatched it up.

"Hello," she barked, still angry.

It was the wrong number, but when Addie May hung up, she knew what to do. As much as she hated to, she would call Teddy Krebs on the telephone.

Addie May found the school directory. Taking a deep breath, she found Teddy's number, then dialed it.

"Hello?" It was a man's voice.

"Hi. Is Teddy there? This is Addie May Jones."

"Well, hello there, Addie May. This is Teddy's dad." Mr. Krebs sounded happy to speak with her. "Teddy's in his room. Hold on a minute."

Addie May heard Mr. Krebs call. "Teddy! It's your girlfriend Addie May!"

Girlfriend? GIRLFRIEND?! *Ew!* Addie May's cheeks turned pink.

There was muffled talking on the other end of the line. Then Teddy got on.

"What do you want?" he said.

Why in the WORLD did Mr. Krebs think she was Teddy's girlfriend anyway? Who gave him that idea? Teddy was always so rude!

"I have a question," Addie May said coldly. "Do you remember the name of the president of Save the Chihuahuas?"

"Sure. Sondra Hopkins."

He remembered! Addie May was impressed in spite of herself. "Can you figure out where she lives?"

"Probably. It ain't rocket science."

Addie May could hear the sneer in Teddy's voice.

"Fine! Talk to me after school then," said Addie May. And then she couldn't resist adding, "When no one is looking."

9

Zack Rust was sitting at the end of the cafeteria table just ahead. He was eating his sack lunch—probably filled with the kind of cool treats Addie May's mother never bought.

"Too expensive!" Mom always said.

Addie May watched the back of Zack's head as she approached his table. She remembered the time he smiled at her in the cafeteria right before Christmas. He didn't have to smile. So why had he? Was he secretly in love with her? Even though he was in the sixth grade and she was in the fourth?

Addie May's heart fluttered.

Closer. Closer.

Not that she was going to sit down by him or anything. She was going to sit at the next table over. Still. He might look up and smile at her as she passed him. What would she do if that happened? Addie May reviewed her options.

1. Pretend she didn't see him. (Safest option.)
2. Smile back. (Riskier option.)
3. Smile back and actually say something. (EXTREMELY risky option! What if he didn't say something back?)

Addie May's heart fluttered even more.

Closer . . .

She was standing right by his side now.

Suddenly, there was a loud noise to her right. Some of the third-grade boys had started wrestling with each other on their way out to recess.

BOOM! Like a tumbleweed made up of arms and legs, those boys bumped straight into Addie May. Her open carton of chocolate milk popped out of her hand . . . and straight into Zack's lap.

"Oh!" Addie May gasped.

Zack jumped up, blinking in surprise.

"Oh! I'm so sorry!"

Zack's friends were laughing. At her. At Zack. Zack grinned back at his friends.

Right now would be a good time for an earthquake to open up the ground and swallow me whole, Addie May thought.

What was the deal with stupid earthquakes anyway? Everyone was always talking about how one day there would be a huge earthquake because Salt Lake City sat on a fault line.

But the earthquakes never happened. Not even when you really, really needed them to, anyway.

Zack began turning toward Addie May. Miserable, Addie May wanted to flee, to hide.

Instead, she looked him straight in the face. And discovered that he was smiling at her! Again!

"Don't worry," he said. "Accidents happen."

Addie May swallowed and nodded, but Zack was already talking to his friends as he wiped himself off.

By the time she sat down, Addie May had

decided that she would marry Zack Rust some-day. If she ever got the chance.

Teddy walked by Addie May's table, carrying his tray. He bumped into her accidentally on purpose.

"Excuse you!" Mimi said loudly from across the aisle.

Teddy didn't answer. But there was a huge scowl on his face.

• • •

"1147 Murphy Avenue," Teddy said when he and Addie May met up after school. Teddy wore a Utah Jazz cap turned sideways on his head.

"What?"

"Sondra Hopkins's address!" Teddy practically spit out the words. "You know. That president lady."

What was going on? Teddy was even grouchier than usual.

"How'd you find it?"

"The phone book, duh," Teddy grumbled. "Why did I ever think you were so smart?"

Addie May blushed. The phone book! Of course! Why hadn't she thought of that?

"Well," Addie May said gruffly, "I think we ought to check her place out."

But how would they get there? Teddy didn't have a bike and it was a long ways to walk. For sure she didn't want to ask for a ride. She could just hear what her parents or Frank would say.

"Why don't we take the bus?" Teddy said.

The bus? Addie May never took the bus. If she had a long distance to go, someone in the family gave her a ride.

"Fine," Addie May said, like she rode the bus forty times a day. "Let's go."

They caught the bus on Third Avenue. When he got on, Teddy flashed a pass at the driver and found a seat. Addie May never took the bus, but it was obvious that Teddy did.

Addie May plunked down her fare, then sat next to Teddy.

The bus was mostly empty. There was a woman with grocery bags, two college students with earphones, and a man brushing his teeth.

Addie May tried not to stare, but she couldn't help herself. The man didn't notice. He was too busy brushing.

"Poor guy," Teddy whispered. "I feel sorry for him every time I see him."

"Me, too," Addie May lied.

Teddy hunched down in his seat. The scowl on his face grew bigger.

"I'm not so sure that Sondra Hopkins has Phantom," he said as the bus bumped along.

"Why not?" Addie May asked. "It all makes perfect sense."

Teddy shrugged. "Maybe. Maybe not."

"So who do you think took your dog?"

Teddy's eyes narrowed. "You won't like my answer."

"Try me."

"Your boyfriend."

Addie May was shocked. Teddy thought she had a boyfriend? A boyfriend who kidnapped Chihuahuas? What kind of a girl did he think she was?

"I do not have a boyfriend," she said stiffly. "Especially not a boyfriend who's a dog stealer."

"Not even fast dogs?"

Addie May looked at Teddy like he was crazy.

"Not even fast dogs that can beat his fast dog in a race this weekend?" Teddy asked.

Was Teddy talking about Phantom and Zack Rust's dog, Tex? Did he think Zack had dognapped Phantom? Worse, did he know that she was in love with Zack Rust? Had he seen her writing Zack's initials and drawing little hearts around them?

Addie May landed a hard punch on Teddy's arm.

"Ouch!" Teddy yelped. "What was *that* for?"

"For being the rudest person I ever met!" Addie May slugged Teddy again, even harder.

The bus grew quiet. Very quiet. The man stopped brushing his teeth and looked at her and Teddy. So did everyone else. Even the bus driver was checking things out in his rearview mirror. For the second time in the same day, Addie May wished the ground would swallow her up whole.

Teddy stared at her. Then he blinked hard and stared out the window instead. He didn't say another word until the bus stopped on the corner of Eleventh and Emerson.

"We're here," Teddy said in a flat voice.

10

It wasn't hard to tell which house belonged to Madame President Sondra Hopkins. It sat apart from the other houses, surrounded by overgrown pine trees. The front porch was littered with leashes and chew toys. The front yard was filled with signs.

SAVE THE CHIHUAHUAS!

POWER TO THE POODLES!

DOGS OF AMERICA UNITE!

FREE CLIFFORD!

Teddy let out a low whistle.

"Wow," said Addie May.

Teddy stuffed his hands into his pockets. "So what do we do next?"

Addie May looked at the house and felt her stomach sink again—this time like an elevator.

She was a girl without a plan. A very NERVOUS girl without a plan.

"Listen to that noise," Teddy said. "It's coming from inside the house."

Addie May held still and heard muffled barking. "It sounds like she's got an entire pet shop in there!"

Addie May's heart began to race. What was going on?

"We need to see what's inside," she said.

Teddy nodded. "Come on. Let's check the windows."

The two of them tiptoed toward the house. Addie May tried not to think about what would happen if Sondra Hopkins suddenly walked outside and caught them snooping around in her yard.

Maybe a talent for snooping wasn't such a great thing after all!

As Addie May and Teddy got close to the house, the barking grew louder. How many dogs were in there anyway? Ten? Fifty? A hundred? Addie May could feel the hair rise on her neck.

She stole a glance at Teddy. Was he scared, too?

Teddy groaned.

"What is it?" Addie May whispered.

"The windows. Look."

Sure enough, the drapes were closed on the front windows.

"Let's see about the back," Addie May said.

Addie May and Teddy picked their way carefully around the side of the house. Chew toys squeaked beneath their feet.

"What is this place?" Teddy asked. "Doggy day care?"

In spite of herself, Addie May smiled.

As they walked around the back of the house,

the barking and yapping grew louder still. Addie May and Teddy looked up at the windows. No luck! The drapes were shut tight in back, too!

"What do we do next?" Teddy asked.

The sneer in his voice was gone. He sounded eager . . . and afraid. Addie May tried to imagine how hard it must be to lose a pet.

"We have to get inside," she said.

"How?"

Addie May stood up straight. The answer was as obvious as looking for Sondra Hopkins's number in the phone book.

"Ring the doorbell!"

11

Addie May and Teddy stood on the front porch, surrounded by water dishes and more chew toys. One thing was for sure. It was NOT going to be easy to come between Sondra Hopkins and her beloved Chihuahuas.

"What if she remembers me?" Teddy asked.

It was a fair question. After all, Teddy had made Sondra Hopkins very angry that day in the park.

"Pull your cap down over your forehead so she can't see your face. She won't remember you," Addie May said, hoping with all her heart that she was right.

Teddy adjusted his cap, reached up, and rang the doorbell.

The sound made the dogs inside go off like fire alarms.

"Don't worry, babies," a voice came from inside. "Mama won't let any bad people hurt you."

Sondra Hopkins threw open the front door. Her frizzy hair stuck out like a pair of angel wings from the side of her head.

"What do you want?" She scowled at Teddy and Addie May as though they were a couple of chew-toy thieves.

Teddy was speechless. Fear gripped Addie May's throat. What should she say?

"We . . . we heard that you have a club for saving Chihuahuas," Addie May choked out. "We want to join."

Sondra Hopkins's face softened. "Oh. Well. I guess you can come in then. I thought you were the neighbors, threatening to turn me in again."

Addie May and Teddy followed Ms. Hopkins into the house. Everywhere Addie May looked, she saw dog things. Dog pictures. Dog calendars. Dog pillows. Dog rugs. Dog statues. Dog lamps.

Dogs.

Addie May counted five Chihuahuas. When she and Teddy sat down on the couch, the Gang of Five sniffed their shoes and barked. Addie May could see Teddy searching for Phantom.

"You sure do have a lot of dogs," Addie May said.

Ms. Hopkins gave her a sly smile. "I have more."

Addie May shivered.

"How many more?" she asked calmly. It was clear Teddy wanted Addie May to do all the talking. That way Ms. Hopkins wouldn't notice him.

"The ones I've saved."

"Saved?" Addie May asked. "From what?"

"Humans, of course!" Ms. Hopkins was so

mad she sprayed spit. "Ever since Chihuahuas started working in those commercials a few years ago, all the wrong people started buying them."

"Who?"

"People with children. People with too much money like all those silly movie stars," said Ms. Hopkins. "People with big feet."

Addie May thought of Frank's feet, which were not only big but stinky as well.

Ms. Hopkins ranted on. "People who dress them up in doll clothes. People who make them run in races."

Teddy looked down at the carpet.

Ms. Hopkins's face glowed. "It's been up to me to save them all!"

"How?" Addie May asked.

"If someone sees a stray Chihuahua running on the street, they call me. I pick the dog up in my special van and bring it here. Lately, though . . ."

Ms. Hopkins stopped and Addie May's scalp began to tingle. It was important to keep Ms. Hopkins talking.

"Go on."

"I don't know if I should." Ms. Hopkins scooped up a small black Chihuahua and kissed its nose.

"Please," said Addie May.

"All right. Since you love Chihuahuas, too, I will." Ms. Hopkins dropped her voice to a whisper. "I've started to rescue dogs from backyards."

Do not look shocked, Addie May told herself.

"People should NOT leave small dogs alone in backyards," said Ms. Hopkins. "It's too dangerous. Someone might come along and steal them."

Yeah, thought Addie May. *Someone like you.*

Just then another little herd of Chihuahuas stampeded into the living room.

Addie May gasped. Could it be? Yes! She was sure of it!

One of them was a chubby Chihuahua she'd seen at the park wearing a clown hat. She recognized him, even though the hat was gone now.

Was Phantom here, too?

Addie May's hands and feet went cold. Sondra Hopkins was a maniac. A Chihuahua-stealing maniac. Why had Addie May dragged Teddy into this house? Who knew what Ms. Hopkins would do to them?

They had to find Phantom. But they also had to get out. Now!

Addie May stood up and yanked Teddy to his feet.

"We gotta go. I just remembered that I have a piano lesson," Addie May lied.

Sondra Hopkins looked disappointed. "But you haven't filled out your membership papers."

"We'll come back," Addie May promised as she and Teddy headed out the front door and toward the street.

Ms. Hopkins and a dozen yapping Chihuahuas followed them onto the front porch. "Wait a minute. I think I've seen you before . . ."

Addie May walked faster. So did Teddy.

"COME BACK HERE!" Ms. Hopkins was screaming now and her dogs were barking. "I KNOW WHO YOU ARE!"

Addie May and Teddy started to run.

"YOU'LL BE SORRY!"

"THAT'S WHAT YOU SAID THE LAST TIME WE MET!" Teddy shouted. Then he and Addie May sprinted for the bus that was just pulling up.

12

"Phew!" said Addie May, flopping down on the bus seat. "That was close!"

Teddy sat next to her, frowning. "Do you think she has Phantom?"

"Yes," said Addie May.

"Me, too."

"I'm sorry we didn't get to look around," said Addie May. "But I had a bad feeling. I wanted to get out."

"Same with me," said Teddy.

"The good news is that Phantom is safe," said Addie May. "The bad news is that you don't have him."

"What should we do next?" asked Teddy.

"I don't know," said Addie May. "Let me think."

The bus bumped along. Addie May looked outside and watched houses stream past her.

"Hey! Wait a minute!" Teddy said. "We're going downtown. We got on the wrong bus."

"That's it!" cried Addie May.

"What's it?"

"My mom's office is downtown! Maybe she'll call her friend Officer Williams to help us."

Teddy looked at Addie May with respect. "Good idea."

In spite of herself, Addie May blushed with pleasure.

• • •

Addie May and Teddy checked in on the fourth floor of the *Deseret News* building. The secretary, Carol, buzzed Addie May's mom.

"You have a couple of visitors." Carol winked at Addie May and Teddy.

A minute later, Mom joined them. She had a pencil tucked behind one ear and a pen behind the other. She had a pair of reading glasses perched on her head and a pair perched on her nose.

Mom was on deadline. Obviously.

"This is Teddy Krebs," Addie May said.

Teddy politely stuck out his hand to shake her mom's. "How do you do?"

Addie May's mouth flew open in surprise. Was *this* really Teddy Krebs? Not Zack Rust dressed up like Teddy Krebs?

"Come back into the newsroom with me," Mom said. "I'm happy you're here—even if I can't chat for long."

Addie May and Teddy trailed Mom into the newsroom, which was filled with people working on computers.

"This won't take long," said Addie May as she and Teddy sat down on chairs by Mom's desk.

"What's going on?" Mom asked, leaning back in her seat.

Addie May and Teddy both started talking at once.

"Hold up," Mom said. "One at a time, please."

Addie May and Teddy took turns telling Mom about their visit to Sondra Hopkins's house. They told her about all the dogs and Ms. Hopkins's special Chihuahua-mobile and the chubby Chihuahua from the park. Addie May watched the smile slip right off Mom's face.

"Did you tell anybody where you were going?" Mom asked sternly.

Slowly, Addie May shook her head no.

"What were you two thinking? It could have been dangerous."

Addie May looked down at her shoes. She felt like she had that time she got caught stealing sugar cookies out of the lunchroom when she was in the first grade.

"It's my fault Addie May went there," said Teddy. "She was just trying to help me find Phantom."

Mom looked at Teddy. Her voice grew softer. "I'm so sorry about your little dog."

"That's why we came!" Addie May's words rushed together. "Can you call Officer Williams and tell him what we saw?"

Mom thought for a minute. "I think that's a good idea, Addie May."

Addie May and Teddy smiled at each other.

"But now I have a deadline to meet. Addie May, I want you to go straight home. Do not pass go. Do not collect two hundred dollars. And, FYI, I am seriously thinking about grounding you for the rest of your life for pulling a stunt like this."

Grounded? Who cared! If Officer Williams found Phantom, it would be worth it!

• • •

The grandfather clock in the entryway chimed again.

Eleven o'clock!

Addie May had been in bed for over an hour. But sleep would not come. She'd start drifting off—but then she'd think of Sondra Hopkins all over again.

For a while Addie May imagined Ms. Hopkins going to jail. Would Officer Williams slap some handcuffs on her like in the movies? The thought made Addie May happy at first.

But then she started wondering about things— like how did a person turn into somebody like Sondra Hopkins, for example?

Why had Ms. Hopkins done what she'd done?

Why did anybody do the things they did?

People were such a mystery!

13

Mom called from work the next day as Addie May walked through the door.

"I talked to Officer Williams," she said. "He wants to meet with me and you and Teddy this afternoon."

"Did he find out anything?"

"The police department sent the people from Animal Services into the Hopkins home. They found dozens of dogs, and he's hoping one of them is Phantom." Mom paused. "I feel sorry for people like Sondra Hopkins, actually. Loneliness can make people do strange things sometimes."

Addie May didn't care about Sondra Hopkins. All she cared about was Phantom. Found! At last! Addie May felt like a kid getting ready to open Christmas presents. Soon, soon Phantom would be home!

"Great!" Addie May shouted into the receiver. "I'm on my way to Teddy's place now. Pick us up there." She gave her mom the address.

"Who's Teddy?" asked Frank as he waltzed into the kitchen. "Your new boyfriend? What happened to ZR?"

Addie May tried to kick him in the shins but missed.

"Say hello to your new lover boy for me!" Frank made kissing noises as Addie May left the room.

• • •

Mr. Covey, the superintendent, was changing a lightbulb in the entryway when Addie May breezed into the apartment building, humming a little song. He smiled down at her from the ladder where he was perched like a friendly bearded parrot.

"Here to see Teddy?" he asked.

Addie May nodded. "I think we've cracked the case, Mr. Covey!"

"Case?"

"You know—the dognapping."

Mr. Covey dropped his lightbulb. It bounced on the carpet and rolled up next to Addie May's shoe.

Mr. Covey gave a nervous laugh. "You get old, you get clumsy." When Addie May handed him the lightbulb, she noticed that his hand was shaking.

"Thanks," he said weakly. "You're a good girl, Addie May."

"See you later, Mr. Covey!" Addie May said as she zipped down the hallway toward Teddy's apartment.

"Teddy!" Addie May squealed. "I think they found Phantom!"

"Yes!" Teddy sounded like he had just slam-dunked a basketball. "This is so great!"

Addie May repeated what Mom had said and laughed. She felt as light as balloons. "I told her to pick us up here because I wanted to give you the news in person. I hope you don't mind."

Teddy turned pink but he still look pleased. "We could play video games or something. I have a big bag of Skittles and some sodas, too."

Video games? Skittles? Sodas? What was going on here? Teddy actually sounded *nice*.

"Sounds fun," Addie May said. And to her surprise, she meant it.

• • •

She looked around, amazed by what she saw. Plants on the windowsill. Pillows on the couch. Framed photos on the bookshelves. True, the apartment was a little messy. Newspapers and shoes were scattered on the floor. A dirty cereal bowl sat with a half-eaten bag of chips on the coffee table in front of the TV. But overall the place had a comfortable feel.

"This is nice," said Addie May.

"Dad and I like it okay." Teddy shrugged. "Do you want a root beer?"

Addie May nodded, then studied the framed photos as Teddy slipped into the kitchen. There were several of Phantom. Phantom licking Teddy's face. Phantom begging for food. Phantom snoozing in a Christmas sock.

When Teddy walked back into the room with two cans of root beer and a bag of Skittles tucked under his arm, Addie May pointed to the picture of Phantom in the stocking.

"This one's my favorite," she said.

Teddy's whole entire face lit up. "Finding Phantom beneath the tree Christmas morning was the best thing that ever happened to me."

Addie May looked at Teddy as though she was meeting him for the very first time. Thank

goodness Phantom would be coming home soon!

Teddy picked up a game control and handed it to Addie May. "You go first."

• • •

As Addie May and Teddy were leaving to meet up with Addie May's mom, they ran into Mr. Covey, who was talking to the Ghost Lady in front of the apartment building. Even though it was warm outside, she wore a baggy gray sweater. Old people dressed like that sometimes because they were always cold. Funny how the fuzzy sweater made the Ghost Lady look so bulky. Normally she was as thin as a pencil.

When the Ghost Lady saw Addie May and Teddy, she whispered goodbye to Mr. Covey and smiled faintly at Addie May. Then she slipped inside like a shadow, her head bowed.

The way the Ghost Lady moved—as though she didn't want to be in anybody's way or even breathe more than her fair share of air—reminded Addie May of a girl in her class who was so shy she turned red whenever anyone looked at her. The girl didn't exactly burst into tears when the teacher called her name. But you could tell she wanted to.

Addie May frowned. Was the Ghost Lady shy? Didn't growing up mean you weren't shy or awkward or lonely anymore? Being lonely must be an awful thing.

Thank goodness Phantom was coming home.

Addie May knew Teddy had been lonely without him.

14

The first thing Addie May noticed when she and Teddy walked with Mom into the lobby of the animal shelter was the smell—an overpowering mix of dog and disinfectant.

The second thing was the noise. A mixed chorus of barking and meowing rose up to greet the visitors.

"Good to see you!" said Officer Williams, stepping forward. He turned to the lady sitting at the front desk, then pointed at Addie May and Teddy. "These are the two junior detectives I was telling you about, Mrs. Hudson."

Mrs. Hudson smiled. "Well done! Thanks to you two, we've been busy reuniting happy dogs with happy owners all over this valley."

Addie May flushed with pride. She saw that Teddy did the same.

"Maybe you ought to get your newspaper to do a story on these two," Officer Williams said to Mom. "Put their pictures on the front page and everything."

Mom grinned. "First things first. Let's find Phantom."

"Good idea," said Mrs. Hudson, standing up. "Why don't you all follow me?"

Mrs. Hudson led the group through large swinging doors and into a room filled with clean crates. There were all kinds of dogs—large and small, purebred and mutt. But mostly there were Chihuahuas. There were so many Chihuahuas that Addie May thought someone should put up a sign saying "Welcome to Chihuahuaville!"

"Imagine having all these dogs in your house at the same time!" Mom said. "Your father would die of a sneeze attack."

"They tell me Sondra Hopkins's place wasn't pretty," Officer Williams replied.

Teddy ignored the conversation. Instead he got right down to work, stopping at the first crate. And then the next. And the next.

Addie May watched Teddy ease his way down the row, peering inside at dog after dog after dog.

When he got to the end, he spun around and faced Mrs. Hudson.

"Are there any more?" Teddy's voice was sharp.

"No," said Mrs. Hudson. "I'm sorry."

Addie May felt sick inside. There just had to be more dogs!

Teddy swallowed hard and started up the row again, searching each crate. "Phantom," he called. "Where are you, boy?"

Addie May's head felt light. The palms of her hands broke out in a sweat. This could not be happening!

She saw Mom and Officer Williams and Mrs. Hudson exchange looks when Teddy joined them.

"No luck?" Officer Williams asked.

Teddy shook his head, then hung it so low that his chin touched his chest. Addie May suspected he was hiding his tears from them.

"Look," said Officer Williams, "I'd really like to help you find your little dog. Assuming he didn't run off—"

"Phantom would never run off!" Teddy was fierce.

Officer Williams tried again. "Assuming he didn't run off, can you think of anyone who might want to take Phantom?"

A picture of the bald man watering his yard and lilac bushes flashed before Addie May's eyes. He'd threatened Teddy. Addie May had heard him with her own ears. Was it possible that he had dognapped Phantom, just to teach Teddy a lesson? Some adults were like that—always trying to teach kids lessons.

"I know!" Addie May shouted.

"I know!" Teddy shouted.

Officer Williams grinned as he nodded at Addie May. "You first."

"Remember your grumpy neighbor? The one who squirted you and Phantom with the garden hose?" she asked Teddy.

Teddy nodded.

"Well, I'll bet you money he knows something!" Addie May was triumphant.

"What do you think?" Officer Williams asked Teddy.

"I was going to say Zack Rust," Teddy said. "Phantom is faster than his dog. I think he was worried that my dog would beat his dog in the race this Sunday. He's right, too."

"Zack Rust!" Addie May exclaimed.

A sneer crept over Teddy's face. When was the last time he had sneered? It had been a while, Addie May realized with a start.

"Zack's dad owns the apartment building," Teddy pointed out. "It would have been easy for somebody to go inside and take my dog if Mr. Rust told him to."

She suddenly felt sick to her stomach. "Mr. Rust isn't a dogsnatcher. Neither is Zack."

"Neither is Zack!" Teddy mimicked Addie May. "Zack's perfect! That's why I love Zack so much."

Teddy turned around and stalked out of the building.

"For your information, I do NOT love Zack Rust." Addie May called after him. She turned to Mom and Officer Williams and added, "I mean it! I do NOT love Zack Rust!"

• • •

It was a really, really, really long ride home.

At first Mom tried to make little jokes, the way she always did when Frank and Addie May were having a fight.

But Addie May and Teddy didn't laugh. Addie May stared out of her window and Teddy stared out of his. Mom sighed and turned up the radio, just in time for a commercial. *Need a car? Then trust Rust!*

Teddy quickly thanked Mom when she pulled up in front of the apartment building. He scuttled out of the car and disappeared inside.

"I hate Teddy Krebs!" Addie May exploded.

Mom glanced over at her. "Why?"

"Because he's so mean!"

"He seems nice to me."

"That's because he doesn't throw dodge balls at your head during recess," Addie May pointed out.

"Does he throw dodge balls at your head?"

"Sometimes."

"Does he throw dodge balls at anybody else's head?" Mom was curious.

Addie May thought about this. "No."

"Hmmmm," said Mom.

"What's that supposed to mean?"

Mom shrugged. "I guess it means you have another mystery to solve. Why does Teddy Krebs throw dodge balls at you, you, and only you?"

"Because he's mean! He's the meanest boy alive!" Addie May said. "I already told you that!"

Mom just laughed as she turned down their street and headed for home.

15

Was Zack Rust a secret dog stealer?

Addie May bit her lower lip as she stood on the sidewalk in front of Zack's gigantic house. She'd found his address in the school directory and pedaled over here early Saturday morning without telling Teddy.

Her plan was to show Phantom's picture to Zack and watch his reaction. Maybe she could even get inside the house and check for telltale signs of Phantom.

Addie May was sure that everything would point to Zack's innocence.

Addie May remembered the way he'd smiled at her the first time in the cafeteria. She remembered the way he'd even smiled at her the second time in the cafeteria—this time covered with chocolate milk! She also remembered the way Zack shook hands with Teddy after the race.

Zack was as kind as he was cute.

But what if Phantom really was being held captive here?

She hadn't thought about this possibility when she'd been at home, still formulating her plan to check out the Rust residence. She'd been so annoyed with Teddy that she'd slammed shut bathroom drawers and bedroom doors as she prepared to leave her house.

"Hey!" Frank had shouted at her. "Take it easy, slugger!"

Now, standing by herself on Zack Rust's front porch, she wondered if she was wrong.

Zack was proud of Tex. That much was obvious. Would he really be capable of dognapping Phantom so that Tex could have a clear shot at winning first place?

If this was the case, Addie May would have to apologize to Teddy—which would be nearly as bad as having to kiss Teddy.

KISS TEDDY?!

Where had THAT idea come from?

Addie May gulped. No point in just standing here. She threw back her shoulders, marched up the front steps, and rang the doorbell.

A pretty woman dressed in a white tennis out-fit opened the big red door. She smiled brightly at Addie May. "Hi there. What can I do for you?"

"Is Zack here?" Addie May's throat felt like it was lined with sandpaper.

The pretty woman nodded. "Come this way."

Addie May followed her to the living room and sat down on a puffy white couch.

"You can wait here while I get him." The pretty woman smiled again. Addie May noticed what perfect, straight teeth she had. They were white, too. As white as the couch.

"Thank you," Addie May said, trying hard not to show her own teeth, which were white but crooked. Too bad she didn't have her braces yet.

"Can I tell him who's here?"

"Addie May Jones. We go to the same school."

"Nice to meet you, Addie May. I'm Zack's mom."

She smiled one last time, then left Addie May alone.

Addie May glanced around the room, which was nothing like Teddy's front room. Everything in this room was white. White rug, white furniture with white pillows, white walls. A bouquet of white roses sat in a vase on the piano. The room was clean and tidy and very beautiful—like a picture in a magazine.

Was there time to search for signs of Phantom before Zack joined her? Addie May leaped to her feet and circled the room, checking under things as she went.

Yip! Yip!

The muffled noise came from beneath a low coffee table, covered with a tablecloth. Could it be Phantom? Dogs had their own barks. Too bad she didn't know Phantom well enough to recognize his.

Addie May dropped to her hands and knees, then stuck her head beneath the table.

"Phantom?" she whispered. "Is that you, boy?"

Addie May was rewarded with sloppy dog kisses all over her face.

"Hi there." It was Zack.

Addie May tried to stand up but banged her head hard.

"Ouch!" she cried.

The dog shot out from beneath the table like a tiny cannonball.

"Hey there, Tex," Addie May heard Zack say.

Tex was settled happily in Zack's arms by the time Addie May stood up and whirled around to face him.

She blushed. "Sorry. I was just trying to—um —to pet him."

Zack gave her an easy smile. "That's okay. Tex just loves to take little naps under there. It's his fort. Did you ever make forts with sheets when you were a little kid?"

Addie May nodded, trying not to feel weak in

the knees. Zack had the most beautiful boy smile ever—as beautiful as his beautiful living room. And here she was! With him! Soon he would be asking her to play video games and they would be laughing and talking. Addie May wondered if he had a big bag of tropical-fruit-flavored Skittles handy.

"You look familiar," Zack said kindly. "What's your name?"

Addie May felt like a balloon with the air whooshing out.

"Addie May Jones."

"You go to my school, right?"

Addie May gave him a weak nod. "I spilled milk all over you in the lunchroom once. It was chocolate."

How stupid could she be? Why did she have to remind him of THAT?

Zack's face lit up. "I remember now!"

Of course he remembered. Who wouldn't?

"Anyway, I came to ask if you've seen this dog." Addie May thrust Phantom's missing-dog poster at Zack. He studied it carefully.

"Yes," he said seriously. "I'm sure I have."

Addie May's heart skipped a beat. She wished she had a tape recorder or a wire tap handy. Zack was getting ready to make a full confession. Obviously.

Zack looked up. "Is this the dog that beat Tex?"

Addie May nodded. This interview wasn't going exactly the way she had hoped it would.

"He's missing?" Zack was shocked. He wasn't faking it, either. Addie May was starting to think Zack wasn't clever enough to fake it. Unlike Teddy, Zack Rust would make a terrible detective.

"He's been missing for days," Addie May said.

"That's terrible!" Zack cried. "I'd die if something happened to Tex."

Tex yipped at the sound of his name and Zack stroked the top of his head. "If I see Phantom, I'll let you know right away."

"Thanks," Addie May said.

She took one last look at Zack's perfect living room.

"Goodbye, Zack," she said as she let herself out the front door.

Goodbye for good.

16

Discouraged, Addie May took one last look at Zack's house and pushed off on her bicycle.

What next?

Should she go to Teddy's apartment and tell him that he'd been wrong about Zack Rust?

A few days ago she would have loved to say *Neener, neener, neener! I was right and you were wrong!* She would have LOVED watching Teddy turn red and choke on the apology stuck in his throat like a fish bone.

But now?

Addie May cringed as she remembered Zack's polite question. *You go to my school, right?*

All this time she'd been drawing little I-love-Zack hearts in her notebook, and he didn't even know she existed. At least Teddy knew who she was.

Addie May remembered something else, too—Mom's words. *Seems to me you have another mystery to solve . . .*

Now what in the world did Mom mean by that? Addie May wondered as she pedaled across the street.

That was the problem with moms. Mostly they told you stuff you didn't want to hear. Do your homework! Pick up your room! Be nice to your brother Frank!

But when you wanted moms to tell you something (such as where they hid your Christmas presents), they never did.

Addie May decided to examine the true facts about Teddy like any good detective and see what they added up to.

Exactly why did Teddy always pick on her? As Addie May thought about this, she remembered he didn't throw dodge balls at anyone else. Not even Mimi, which was strange, because if anybody deserved to have a dodge ball chucked at her head, it was Mimi.

Not only that, but Teddy never really caused trouble in class. Not like some of the other boys. He didn't speak out of turn or throw erasers when Mrs. Barnson looked the other way.

Does he pick on me because he thinks I'm stupid? Addie wondered. *Then why did he ask me to help him find Phantom?*

The true facts about Teddy added up to a big fat huge zero. Nothing made sense.

A car honked its horn at her. Addie May swerved and almost toppled off her bike.

"Watch where you're going!" a lady shouted at her from an open window.

Addie May stopped and took a deep breath.

Time to stop thinking about Teddy and start paying attention to traffic!

• • •

In the end, Addie May decided to ride over to Teddy's house and tell him the news about Zack in person.

As she approached the apartment building, Addie May noticed the fat bald man in front of his house again. This time, instead of spraying the lawn with his garden hose, he was sitting on the front porch, holding a cat. The bald man wore a T-shirt that said I ♥ PERSIAN CATS.

Addie May slowed down and watched as the man gently combed the cat's long white fur.

"Nice Fluffy," he said.

Fluffy looked up at the bald man with adoring eyes and blinked.

No wonder he'd sprayed the hose at Phantom! He didn't want Phantom chasing Fluffy around the yard. He probably didn't want Phantom chasing Fluffy inside the house either.

So much for the idea that the bald man had kidnapped Phantom to teach Teddy a lesson.

"That sure is a pretty cat you have there," Addie May called out.

The man looked up and grinned.

It was just amazing what a smile could do to a grumpy guy's face!

17

Addie May locked up her bike on the rack in front of the apartment building and pushed open the door.

Yip!

Addie May froze in her tracks and held her breath as the door swung shut behind her.

Yip! Yip!

No doubt about it. There was a dog. A small dog. Somewhere in this building!

Had Teddy found Phantom?

Quivering with excitement, Addie May raced to Teddy's apartment and pounded on the door. She half expected to hear Phantom bark out a greeting.

Teddy opened the door a crack, the TV set blaring behind him. Addie May was surprised he'd even heard her knock.

"What do you want?" His voice was hostile.

"Did you find Phantom?" Addie May shouted over the noise.

"Is that supposed to be some kind of a sick joke?"

Addie May was as surprised as if she'd just been hit in the head by a dodge ball.

"But I thought I heard him . . ." Her voice trailed off.

Teddy opened the door a little wider, although he still didn't invite her to come inside.

"You heard Phantom?" he asked.

"I don't know," said Addie May, feeling confused, like she did sometimes when she woke up from a long nap and couldn't remember if it was today or tomorrow. "I thought I did. Didn't you hear something?"

Stupid question. Of course Teddy hadn't heard anything. The TV set was on too loud.

"I'm sorry," she said. "I wasn't trying to play a trick on you. Honest."

She and Teddy stood there without saying anything. Finally, Teddy pushed the door wide open. Addie May stepped inside as he turned down the TV.

"Where did the noise come from?" Teddy asked.

"I wasn't paying attention. I just assumed it came from your place."

"Maybe we should walk up and down the halls," Teddy said.

"Good idea," Addie May said. "You take the first floor, I'll take the second."

Teddy looked down at his shoes. "I was thinking we could walk together."

• • •

Addie May and Teddy had been prowling through the hallway for less than five minutes when they heard a faint *yip* at the end of the hallway on the first floor.

"That came from Mr. Covey's apartment," Teddy said, his face grim.

Addie May nodded, feeling a little sick to her stomach.

Why did sweet Mr. Covey have to be the bad guy?

"What should we do?" Addie May asked.

For a split second she wondered if they should call Officer Williams. Mr. Covey didn't seem dangerous. But then again, he hadn't seemed like a dognapper either.

Addie May and Teddy walked up to Mr. Covey's door. They heard voices inside the apartment, arguing.

Teddy knocked. Again they heard the sound of a small dog barking. Addie May felt a stab of excitement and fear.

"Who's there?" Mr. Covey called.

"Teddy Krebs," Teddy answered in a strong, clear voice. Addie May was impressed with Teddy's grownup manner in spite of herself.

Again the *yips*! Again the voices.

Mr. Covey finally opened the door.

And a tiny dog with one floppy ear streaked across the floor and leaped straight into Teddy's arms.

18

P hantom!" Teddy squealed.

Phantom smothered Teddy's face with kisses. Teddy laughed and gulped for air. "Where have you been hiding out, boy?"

Addie May looked from Teddy to Mr. Covey, who was smiling broadly. It was then that she realized she and Teddy were not alone with Mr. Covey in his apartment.

The Ghost Lady! She was sitting behind Mr. Covey, twisting a lacy handkerchief. Her small wrinkled face was as unhappy as Teddy's face was happy. There was something else on her face, too.

Fear.

Addie May remembered the strangely bulky sweater on the Ghost Lady yesterday, and suddenly she knew exactly where Phantom had been for the past few days.

Addie May saw Mr. Covey look quickly over his shoulder at the Ghost Lady, who hung her head.

Mr. Covey cleared his throat. "He's been here, Teddy, keeping me company. I'm sorry. I should have told you sooner."

"That's not true," Addie May said. "Phantom hasn't been here."

The Ghost Lady sighed and looked straight at Addie May. "You're right, of course." Then she turned to Mr. Covey. "No need to protect me, Irwin."

"Lilah . . ." Mr. Covey said, but the Ghost Lady shook her head firmly.

She stood up and shuffled slowly over to Teddy. When she was close enough, Phantom squirmed around and gave her a kiss, too. Right on the chin. The Ghost Lady—Lilah—smiled and tickled Phantom behind the ears. For a split second, Addie May could see the girl Lilah had been a long time ago.

"I owe you an apology," she said gravely to Teddy. "Phantom has been with me."

Her confession hung in the air like a bomb ready to drop.

She went on. "I found him in the hall on Wednesday when you and your father were gone.

111

I scratched his tummy and gave him a piece of my peanut butter cookie. Before I knew it, he'd followed me back to my apartment."

Phantom's tail wagged at the sound of Lilah's whispery voice.

"I planned to return him as soon as you got home from school, but he was such good company." Lilah smiled at Phantom. "He snuggled right up next to me when I sat down to watch my programs on the television. It felt so good to have him by my side that I made myself believe you and your father wouldn't miss him for just one night . . ."

The nerve of some people! Addie May fumed.

"Of course Teddy missed him!" Addie May turned to Teddy. "You probably cried yourself to sleep that night and every night, right?"

Teddy blushed. "Duh. I do not cry myself to sleep!"

He was lying. Obviously. Addie May could tell.

Lilah went on. "Wednesday turned into Thursday. Thursday turned into Friday. And here it is—Saturday morning." She shook her head.

Addie May whirled around and stared down Mr. Covey. "Did you know about this?"

"After you asked me if Phantom was still on

the couch when I left Teddy's apartment, I started wondering about it myself." Mr. Covey stroked his white beard thoughtfully. "I could have sworn he was. But suddenly I wasn't so sure. I had to accept the possibility that he could have left the apartment while I was working on the disposal."

"Phantom does like to sneak away sometimes," Teddy said.

"Irwin came to each of our apartments, asking if we'd seen Phantom," said Lilah. "I told him I hadn't. But he heard Phantom bark in my bedroom."

"I had no idea you were so lonely, Lilah," he said. "You should have called me. We could play gin rummy together. I play a mean game of gin rummy."

"EXCUSE ME! AND ALSO, WAIT A MINUTE!" Addie May said. "LONELINESS IS NOT AN EXCUSE FOR STEALING DOGS! STEALING DOGS IS NOT ACCEPTABLE BEHAVIOR!"

Even if you're a little old lady whom nobody suspects, she almost added.

Phantom was so startled by Addie May's loud voice, he almost jumped out of Teddy's arms. Lilah looked at Addie May, and then she looked at Teddy.

"Your friend is right," Lilah said to Teddy. "Stealing dogs is not acceptable behavior. I wouldn't blame you if you called the police."

Addie May tried to picture what Lilah would look like wearing handcuffs while sitting in the back of Officer Williams's squad car. She tried to imagine the headlines in the *Deseret News*.

DOGNAPPER NABBED!

CHIHUAHUA THIEF FOUND BARKING UP THE WRONG TREE!

"Teddy, I don't expect you to forgive me. I certainly don't expect you to believe me when I say I've never done anything like this before." Lilah closed her eyes and remembered. "The last time I took something that wasn't mine was in the second grade. I borrowed a piece of colored chalk from our teacher right before recess and forgot to give it back."

Lilah opened her eyes and pulled her light gray

sweater tightly around her hunched shoulders. "I do want you to know how terribly, terribly sorry I am, Teddy."

She hung her head again, like a second grader waiting to be sent to the principal's office.

Teddy looked at her and then he shrugged. "Don't worry about it. Everybody makes mistakes."

He dropped a quick kiss on the top of Phantom's head—just like he had that day in the park. Only this time he didn't care who saw him.

Addie May was stunned! STUNNED! Where was the Teddy Krebs who threw dodge balls at her head and called her names? Had space aliens abducted him and left this Teddy Krebs clone in his place?

Lilah looked up in surprise, then gave Teddy's clone a grateful smile.

"You have a good heart, son," Mr. Covey said, and Addie May could have sworn there were tears in his eyes. Or maybe it was just the light.

"Good thing he didn't stay with you any longer, though," Teddy said to Lilah. "Look at his belly. He's getting too fat to run."

Phantom barked and everyone laughed. Even Lilah.

Especially Lilah.

19

The day of the Chihuahua Race did NOT dawn bright and clear.

In fact, it was raining cats and dogs. Or, as Mr. Krebs said—it was raining cats and Chihuahuas.

Still, the weather did not stop hordes of people from showing up with their little dogs, many of them in soggy costumes. Addie May arrived with Frank and their parents. Teddy arrived with Phantom, Mr. Krebs, Mr. Covey, and Lilah, who wore a scarf that was pink! Not gray!

Zack was there with his parents and Tex, too. When he saw Addie May and Teddy, he gave them both a friendly wave.

Addie May smiled. The thing about Zack was that he was really nice. A little lean in the brain department. But nice. A guy like that would make a good boyfriend, probably.

Too bad she was over him.

Zack's dad, Bobby Rust, was the honorary master of ceremonies. He stood before the wet crowd and welcomed them to the event.

"And now," he said in a booming voice, "let the Chihuahua races begin!"

There were a lot of preliminary heats. Both Phantom and Tex easily won their races, beating out (among others) a Chihuahua in a tutu and another dressed like Elvis. Addie May, Mr. Krebs, Mr. Covey, and Lilah cheered as they shared Lilah's homemade chocolate chip cookies.

Then came the next round of heats: six races for the dogs who had won their first race. Again, Phantom and Tex took on and beat all challengers.

"And now for the semifinals!" Mr. Rust announced. "This sure is getting exciting, folks!"

Not as exciting as scoping out Sondra Hopkins's house, Addie May thought, *but definitely a lot more fun.*

Soon there were two races left. Phantom ran in the first race and won. Tex ran in the second race and won.

At last! Time for the final showdown!

Addie May watched as Teddy shook Zack's

hand before putting Phantom in the chute. Teddy Krebs was a mystery, for sure.

Addie May remembered Mom's words. *Why does Teddy Krebs throw dodge balls at you, you, and you only?*

Why was he so mean to her? Especially when he almost seemed to like her at times? She remembered the way they had laughed together when playing video games and eating Skittles.

"Chihuahuas, on your mark . . ." shouted Mr. Rust.

Addie May could see both Teddy and Zack whispering last words of encouragement to their dogs.

"Get set . . ."

Teddy looked up and searched the crowd. What was he looking for? Addie May waved and Teddy smiled.

He'd been looking for her. Addie May Jones.

"GO!"

Ah ha! Addie May thought. *Another mystery solved . . .*

• • •

Phantom and Tex streaked down their lanes. Just as in the first race, Tex took an early lead, but Phantom soon closed the gap between them.

The crowd went wild.

Lilah ripped the pink scarf from her neck and began waving it like a flag. "Go, Phantom! Go!"

Mom, Mr. Krebs, and Mr. Covey were jumping up and down. So was Dad, between sneeze attacks. Even Frank was cheering.

"WATCH OUT FOR THE RAT CATCHER!" Frank shouted.

Phantom and Tex ran neck and neck. *Just like thoroughbred horses,* Addie May thought. *Really, really, ridiculously small thoroughbred horses.*

Faster and faster. Closer and closer.

Who would win the race?

At the very last possible second, Tex pulled away.

"AND THE WINNER IS . . . TEX!" Mr. Rust bellowed into the microphone.

"Oh my," said Lilah. "It looks like Phantom ate too many peanut butter cookies at my house."

The crowd cheered happily as Zack picked up Tex and held him high for everyone to see. Tex pricked his ears up and barked.

What would Addie May see on Teddy's face as he shook Zack's hand? Disappointment? Frustration? Jealousy? Addie May almost hated to look.

Slowly she took her eyes from Zack and found Teddy. Who was smiling. She could see him mouth the words "Good boy!" over and over again as Phantom snuggled up against Teddy's chest.

"I guess there are some things more important than winning, after all," Mr. Covey whispered in Addie May's ear.

20

That night, Addie May took her pen collection out of her top drawer. Then she borrowed a piece of Mom's fanciest stationery. She also found some matches, a stick of lavender sealing wax, and her own personal stamp with the letter "A" for Addie.

Time to write a note. Addie May selected her favorite gel pen—the orange one—and began printing.

Dear Teddy,

I am writing you this letter to tell you that it is NOT cool to throw dodge balls at a girl's head just because you happen to be in love with her.

There are better ways of communicating.

Sincerely yours,
Addie May Jones

She tried to imagine Teddy's reaction when he read the note. He'd probably rip it up and throw it in the garbage can. And then he'd never speak to her again. Ever. Not in a billion, trillion years.

Would she like it if Teddy never spoke to her again?'

Addie May sighed and looked at her note. Such a waste of beautiful orange gel pen.

She crumpled up the piece of stationery and threw it into the garbage can. Perfect rim shot!

Frank would be so proud.